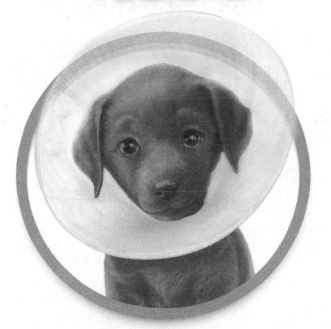

Scaredy-Dog

Lucy Daniels

STORY ONE:
Dog Detectives

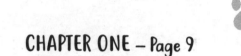

ANIMAL ARK

Scaredy-Dog

With special thanks to Caryn Jenner

To LXL

Illustrations by Jo Anne Davies for Artful Doodlers

ORCHARD BOOKS

First published in Great Britain in 2019 by The Watts Publishing Group

1 3 5 7 9 10 8 6 4 2

Text copyright © Working Partners Limited, 2019
Illustrations copyright © Working Partners Limited, 2019

The moral rights of the author and illustrator have been asserted.

A CIP catalogue record for this book
is available from the British Library.

ISBN 978 1 40835 418 6

Printed and bound in Great Britain by CPI Group (UK) Ltd, Croydon, CR0 4YY

The paper and board used in this book are made from wood from responsible sources.

Orchard Books
An imprint of
Hachette Children's Group
Part of The Watts Publishing Group Limited
Carmelite House
50 Victoria Embankment
London EC4Y 0DZ

An Hachette UK Company
www.hachette.co.uk
www.hachettechildrens.co.uk

STORY TWO:
Puppy Hero

STORY ONE:
Dog Detectives

CHAPTER ONE

Amelia Haywood gave a little bone-shaped biscuit to the spotty Dalmatian crouched obediently at her feet. "Don't worry," she told the shaggy English sheepdog next to him, who looked up at her with round, pleading eyes. "I haven't forgotten you!"

Amelia couldn't stop smiling. It was Dog Day at Animal Ark. She and her best friend, Sam, were in the reception area, handing out treats to the dogs and information sheets to their owners, with tips on canine care. The morning sun streamed in through the window.

Amelia was glad it was the school

holidays. Now that she and Sam were the veterinary surgery's official young helpers, they would get to spend a whole week with the animals. It was going to be brilliant!

Mac, Sam's West Highland terrier puppy, darted out from behind a lanky whippet. His stubby tail wagged as he licked Amelia's hand.

Amelia laughed. "Is Mac allowed another biscuit?" she asked Sam.

Sam rolled his eyes. "Just one more!"

"Sit," said Amelia. She'd helped Sam to train the puppy and she was pleased to see that Mac sat obediently. "Good boy," she said, giving him the treat.

Amelia looked up as a tall, strong-looking man entered, carrying a German shepherd in his arms. He had short grey hair and a worried look on his face. Amelia saw that a patch of fur on his dog's foreleg was matted with blood. *Oh, no,* she thought, hurrying to close the door behind him. *This can't be good …*

Mr Hope, one of the vets, crossed the reception, smiling kindly. "Hello," he said to the man. "I don't believe we've met before. What's happened here?"

The man nodded a greeting. "I'm Kent Jacobs. I've only just moved to Welford." The man stroked the dog's head gently. "And this is Sherlock … He went to explore some bushes near our new cottage and came out with this wounded leg. I've no idea how it happened."

Mr Hope turned to Amelia and Sam. "Do you two want to help me in the consulting room?"

Amelia and Sam nodded. "Yes, please!"

Julia, the receptionist, steered her

wheelchair around her desk. "I'll keep an eye on Mac," she told Sam, winking. "He can help me hand out the treats — that's if he doesn't scoff them all first!"

"Thanks, Julia," said Sam, as he and Amelia followed Mr Hope.

In the consulting room, they watched as Mr Hope and Mr Jacobs gently laid the German shepherd on the examination table. Sherlock had a mixture of brown and black fur, a long nose and pointy ears. Amelia knew that German shepherds were particularly calm and intelligent dogs. *Even though they look really fierce!*

Sure enough, Sherlock was patient as

Mr Hope used a tweezer to move some of the bloody fur away so he could get a better look at the wound. A trickle of blood dripped on to the examining table.

Amelia leaned forwards so she could see better. *I've got to learn as much as possible if I'm going to become a vet one day,* she thought as she watched.

Mr Hope cut away some of the matted fur on Sherlock's leg. Then he gently cleaned the blood off with a cotton pad, which Amelia knew was soaked in hydrogen peroxide to kill any germs that might give Sherlock a nasty infection.

Now Amelia could see the wound clearly. She gasped. There were two small holes in the dog's skin!

Mr Hope gave a low whistle. "It looks like Sherlock's been bitten!" he said.

"Bitten?" said Mr Jacobs, frowning. "How strange!"

"By a fox?" asked Sam.

"Or a badger?" asked Amelia.

"Actually, I'm pretty sure it was another dog," said Mr Hope. "Luckily, the wound isn't too deep."

"Wow," said Sam. "Sherlock's a big dog. The dog that bit him must be really tough!"

Mr Hope finished cleaning the wound and rubbed on some antibacterial ointment. Sherlock just licked his lips nervously.

"Dogs don't usually bite, and when they do it's often because they're scared," said Mr Hope. "Amelia, can you please pass me that bandage?

Amelia reached for the supplies at the end of the table, handing one to the vet.

She leaned down over the German shepherd, who was calm and still as Mr Hope applied the bandage.

"Nearly done, Sherlock," she whispered. She looked up at Mr Jacobs, who was softly stroking his dog's head. "He's very calm."

"Well, he's a retired police dog," said Mr Jacobs. "His job was to sniff out suspected criminals, so he's used to stressful situations."

Sam's eyes lit up with excitement. "A crime-fighting dog? Awesome!"

"Very cool!" agreed Amelia. "How did Sherlock learn to do that?"

"I trained him myself," said Mr Jacobs, proudly. "Training police dogs used to be my job. Then I retired and moved here. I just bought Scarecrow Cottage."

"That place down by the village shop?" Sam asked.

Mr Jacobs nodded.

"Well," Amelia said, frowning, "I think the dog that bit Sherlock could use some training."

"Hmmm," said Sam thoughtfully. "I wonder who the mystery biter is?"

CHAPTER TWO

When Amelia and Sam finished their
morning shift at Animal Ark, they
walked along the wooded path to the
Old Mill Bed and Breakfast, where Sam
and his parents lived.

"My Auntie Jen phoned last night,"
Sam told Amelia. He'd taken Mac off

the lead, and the little Westie scampered ahead, sniffing at the patches of bluebells along the way. "She's got to go on a business trip for a week, so we get to look after her puppy, Coco, while she's away!"

Amelia felt a buzz of excitement at the thought of meeting a new puppy. "Can I help?" she asked.

"Of course!" said Sam.

They ran after Mac all the way to the Old Mill. As soon as Sam pulled the door open, a dark brown puppy bounded towards them from the kitchen. Mac and the puppy started yapping at each other.

"Coco!" called a woman who Amelia guessed was Auntie Jen. She looked quite similar to Sam's dad, with dark, curly hair and a friendly face.

"This must be Coco!" said Amelia.

Auntie Jen scooped up her puppy. Coco was a chocolate Labrador, with smooth brown fur and bright eyes, little ears that flopped over and a tail that wagged energetically.

"Mac, sit," Sam said. Immediately, the little white Westie sat at his feet. "Good dog." Sam pulled a treat from his pocket and crouched down to give it to Mac.

Coco jumped out of Auntie Jen's arms and raced over to Sam, pawing at his pocket.

"Coco, sit," said Sam. But Coco ignored him.

"I've only just started training her," said Auntie Jen. "And now I've been called away on this business trip! Such terrible timing."

Sam's eyes widened. "We can train her for you!"

"Just like we trained Mac!" added Amelia.

Auntie Jen smiled. "I suppose you can have a go."

The two dogs sniffed each other and wagged their tails.

Sam laughed. "They're making friends already."

Just then, they heard a car horn beep in the drive.

"Jen," called Mr Baxter, coming into the hall, "that's your taxi."

Auntie Jen leaned down to give Coco a kiss. "Be good, Coco."

She gave quick hugs to everyone else, even Amelia, then hurried outside with her suitcase to catch her taxi.

They all waved to Auntie Jen from the door as the taxi drove away.

"We'll have to keep Coco away from the mystery biter," said Amelia, as they turned back into the B&B.

Sam frowned. "That could be tricky … After all, we don't know who it is!"

"Who wants some chocolate cake?" called Sam's mum from the kitchen. "Jen brought it to say thank you."

Amelia and Sam grinned at each other. "Me, please!" said Sam.

They all gathered in the kitchen,

around a chocolate cake covered with a dark, fudgy frosting. Mrs Baxter cut pieces of cake and put them on plates.

Amelia took a bite. "It's amazing!" she said, through a mouthful of cake.

As the others were nodding in agreement, Coco suddenly climbed up on to the table. She slid on her belly, her little paws splayed out to the sides.

"Coco, no!" said Mrs Baxter, making a grab. But the puppy scrambled out of the way, knocking the cake to the floor. Splat! Fudgy frosting spattered everywhere. Coco dived down into the chocolate mess.

"Oh, no!" gasped Amelia. She reached out for the little puppy. "Here, Coco!" But Coco sped past her, stepping in a big splodge of chocolate frosting.

Barking happily, Coco dashed out of the kitchen, treading chocolatey pawprints as she went.

"Stop her!" called Sam.

CHAPTER THREE

The puppy darted into the hall and up the stairs, leaving a trail of dark brown pawprints on the carpet. Amelia and Sam chased after Coco, with Mr and Mrs Baxter following close behind.

"What's this? Not another mischievous puppy?" said a deep voice.

A burly bald man was standing on the landing, hands on hips.

Coco stopped a couple of steps below Mr Ferguson and looked up at him, as if deciding what to do next.

Oh no! thought Amelia. Mr Ferguson was a regular guest at the B&B, and he could be quite grumpy.

"Don't worry, Mr Ferguson. Coco won't—" began Sam. But before he could finish, Coco leapt up on to Mr Ferguson, smearing chocolatey pawprints all over his jeans!

"Little rascal!" shouted Mr Ferguson.

Sam pounced on Coco and scooped her up in his arms. "Sorry, Mr

Ferguson," he said.

"This place is overrun with animals!" huffed Mr Ferguson. "First Mac, and now this one." He looked annoyed, but he gave Coco's ears a  quick ruffle all the same, before striding down the corridor to his room.

"There's chocolate everywhere!" said Mr Baxter.

"What a silly girl you are," Amelia told Coco, as she gently stroked the puppy's brown nose.

Suddenly, Amelia spotted a smudge of chocolate frosting in the corner of Coco's mouth. "Oh no!" She looked at Sam in alarm. "Coco ate some of the cake."

"But chocolate is poisonous to dogs!" said Sam.

Amelia's heart sank. *I hope Coco isn't ill!*

"We'd better go to the vet – quick!" said Mrs Baxter. "We'll leave Mac here."

Mrs Baxter led them out to the car and hopped into the driver's seat. Amelia and Sam climbed into the back, holding Coco.

"I'm doing a terrible job looking after

Coco," said Sam sadly, as his mum drove off. "I've only been looking after her for five minutes and we're already taking her to Animal Ark!"

"It's not your fault," said Amelia. She stroked the puppy's soft head on the seat between them. "I'm sure Coco's going to be fine."

She wasn't sure if she quite believed it, though.

At Animal Ark, Dog Day was still in full swing. Sam carried Coco through the crowd of dogs and their owners to the reception desk. Amelia and Mrs Baxter were right behind him.

Julia smiled at them. "Back so soon? Have you brought another puppy for Dog Day?"

Sam shook his head. "Coco's eaten some chocolate," he told her.

"Oh dear," said Julia, suddenly serious. "You'd better take her straight through."

They hurried down the corridor to the examining room, where Mrs Hope, the other vet at Animal Ark, was saying goodbye to a man with a cat in a wicker carrier.

"Hello! Who've we got here?" asked Mrs Hope.

"This is my Auntie Jen's puppy, Coco," said Sam, setting the little dog down on the examining table. "We think she ate some chocolate."

Mrs Hope frowned. "How much did she eat, and when?"

"We're not sure," said Amelia. "It was about twenty minutes ago. We came as soon as we realised."

Coco was looking around curiously, wagging her tail. There didn't seem to be anything wrong with her.

Mrs Hope nodded. "It's good you brought her in. She seems fine now, but it takes a while for the symptoms of chocolate poisoning to appear, so the sooner she's treated, the better."

"Do you think she needs to be sick?" asked Sam, looking a little queasy at the thought.

"Exactly," said Mrs Hope, preparing some medicine in a dropper. "Just to be on the safe side."

Amelia spread a mat on the floor. Then she and Sam held Coco still on

the table, while Mrs Hope opened Coco's mouth and squeezed the medicine in. Coco squirmed and whined, trying to get away.

"This medicine's going to make you vomit, Coco," Mrs Hope told the puppy. "So any chocolate that you've eaten will come out before it has a chance to get into your system and do any damage."

Mrs Hope set Coco down on the mat. The little puppy let out a high-pitched whine. Then she gagged, and threw up on the mat. She pawed the mat, then threw up again.

"Good girl!" Amelia told her. "Urgh –

it's horrible being sick, isn't it?"

"You might be a chocolate Lab," said Sam, "but you still shouldn't *eat* chocolate."

Coco threw up a few more times. Then she looked up at everyone and barked, her tail wagging.

Mrs Hope lifted Coco back on to the examining table and listened to the puppy's heart with a stethoscope. "Her heartbeat isn't too fast. That's good. Just look out for signs of diarrhoea, panting and hyperactivity."

Coco barked again. She batted the stethoscope out of Mrs Hope's hand with her paw and leapt from the examining table on to the desk, scattering a pile of papers.

"She's certainly energetic, isn't she?" said Mrs Hope, as Sam caught Coco by her collar. "That's what I mean by hyperactivity. It can be a sign of chocolate poisoning."

"This is normal for Coco!" said Sam, holding the puppy in his arms. "That's how she knocked over the chocolate cake in the first place. Auntie Jen was going to start training her, but she had to go away on business."

"Hey, didn't Mr Jacobs say that he was a dog trainer?" said Amelia. "Maybe we could ask him to help us with Coco!"

Mrs Hope gave her a smile. "That's a brilliant idea! Actually, we've got quite a few puppies registered at Animal Ark who could use some training."

"Let's do it!" said Sam.

"Maybe we can even figure out who the mystery biter is," said Amelia, as they left the surgery.

While Mrs Baxter took Coco back to the Old Mill, Amelia and Sam decided to go and talk to Mr Jacobs. Sam knew where Scarecrow Cottage was.

"Is it a scary place?" Amelia asked, as they approached the village shop.

Sam laughed. "Only if you're a crow!"

As they passed the village shop, they saw three girls sitting together on the bench outside, eating ice lollies. With a sinking heart, Amelia recognised Tiffany's long brown ponytail. The other girls were her friends, Chloe and Mia. On Tiffany's back, Amelia could see the doggy backpack that she used to carry

Sparkle, her Bichon Frise puppy. The little white creature gazed through the mesh window of the doggy backpack.

Tiffany was gesturing so much, Amelia thought her ice lolly might go flying. "It's going to be brilliant!"

"What is?" asked Amelia, startling Tiffany, who spun round. Poor Sparkle gave a yelp.

Sparkle clearly doesn't like being stuffed in the backpack! thought Amelia.

"Tiffany's party tomorrow," said Chloe. "Aren't you guys coming?"

Tiffany rolled her eyes as she ate the last bite of her lolly. "I suppose they can come."

"Tiffany says there's going to be an enormous cake," said Mia.

Chloe nodded eagerly. "And fireworks!"

With a heavy sigh, Tiffany handed Amelia and Sam two sparkly pink invitations from her pocket. "My parents said I have to invite everyone in our class."

"Fireworks?" said Amelia. "But what about Sparkle? Dogs can get really stressed by loud noises."

"Whatever," said Tiffany. She snatched back the invitations. "If you're going to be losers then don't bother coming."

"Suits me," Sam whispered, as he and Amelia carried on past the shop. "Hey, why don't you come over to my house tomorrow instead? We can have our own party."

Amelia smiled. "Great idea!"

Just then, they heard the roar of a motorbike, and Mr Ferguson rode past on his gleaming Harley-Davidson. As the loud noise faded, Amelia could hear a frightened whimper. She turned around and saw Sparkle squirming in the backpack, scrabbling at the mesh with his paws as if he desperately wanted to get out.

Uh oh ...

"Sparkle really doesn't like loud noises," Amelia said to Sam. "I hope Tiffany cancels the fireworks."

"And ruin her own party?" Sam laughed, but his expression was sad. "I don't think so."

CHAPTER FOUR

Amelia and Sam soon arrived at
Scarecrow Cottage, where Mr Jacobs
lived. He was slowly walking Sherlock
around the front garden. The big
German shepherd was limping on his
bandaged foreleg, but his furry tail was
still wagging.

"He was desperate to get outside," Mr Jacobs explained, when he noticed the children at the gate.

"Oh, I hope he's back to normal soon!" said Amelia. "Mr Jacobs … we wanted to talk to you about dog training."

"What would you like to know?" Mr Jacobs asked.

"My Auntie Jen's puppy is staying with us this week," explained Sam.

"And Coco really needs some training!"

"Mrs Hope says that there are other puppies registered at Animal Ark too," said Amelia. "We were thinking, maybe we could train them all together."

"I'd be happy to run a puppy training course," said Mr Jacobs, rubbing his chin. "Usually they take place once a week over a few months, but if Coco is only staying with you this week, then maybe we should try an intensive week-long course."

"That would be brilliant!" said Sam. His brown eyes shone with excitement. "We'll ask Julia at Animal Ark to get in touch with some other puppy owners."

"Where would we hold the classes?" Amelia asked Mr Jacobs.

"It should be somewhere with plenty of space for lively pups, but enclosed so they can't run off," said Mr Jacobs.

They all thought for a moment.

"I know!" said Amelia. "What about the outdoor basketball court at Welford Sports Centre? It has a really tall fence around it."

"What do you think, Mr Jacobs?" asked Sam.

"It sounds perfect," he said.

Amelia and Sam grinned. They waved goodbye to Mr Jacobs and turned to head home.

But as they passed a row of bushes, Sam stopped. "That must be where Sherlock got bitten," he said.

"I guess you're right," said Amelia, frowning.

Amelia was about to move on when she noticed something tangled among the stems. It was a blue ribbon. The colour looked strangely familiar. "I've seen that before," she muttered.

I just can't think where …

The very next day, Amelia and Sam brought Coco to the basketball court. Mr Jacobs was already there with Sherlock, who still had a bandage on his leg. Coco barked and strained at her lead, trying to get Sherlock's attention. But the older dog stayed obediently by Mr Jacobs's side.

"I hope some other puppies turn up," said Amelia.

"I'm sure they will," said Mr Jacobs. "Good dog owners know how important training is."

Soon, the other puppies started arriving with their owners. Everyone introduced themselves and their dogs. There was a big St Bernard puppy

called Casey, belonging to a teenage boy called Theo. Then came JJ, a long sausage dog, with Mr Fanelli who worked at the library; Dexter, a tall Great Dane with a lady called Dina; and lastly, a little pug called Pixie with Mrs Shah, who was friends with Amelia's gran.

Coco got very excited seeing all the other puppies. She tried to join in as Dexter and Casey jumped up and barked at each other. Meanwhile, JJ and Pixie chased each other around the basketball court.

"Welcome to puppy training class," said Mr Jacobs. "Let's get started, shall

we? First,
we're going to
practise recall.
I'll demonstrate
with Sherlock."
He walked to the
other end of the court.
"Sherlock!" he called. Sherlock
looked at him. "Here!"

The German shepherd immediately
trotted across the basketball court.

"Good dog, Sherlock," said Mr Jacobs,
giving him a pat. "It's important to
reward dogs when they do something
correctly. For puppies, the reward is
normally a treat, but do give lots of

cuddles, too. Recall takes practice. Sherlock has been doing this for several years now, so he knows exactly what to do!"

Mr Jacobs smiled. "Now it's your turn to practise. First, use your dog's name to get their attention. Then give the command."

Theo went to the other end of the basketball court first.

"Casey, here!" he called.

The St Bernard puppy scampered towards Theo, but got distracted and stopped halfway.

"See if he'll come if you move a bit closer," suggested Mr Jacobs.

Theo moved closer, holding out the treat. "Casey! Here!"

This time, the big St Bernard pup raced towards Theo and knocked him over in his eagerness to get the treat.

Everyone laughed.

"It's a good start," said Mr Jacobs. "Next time, wait until Casey's calm before giving the reward."

Next, it was JJ the dachshund's turn. She went to her owner first time. So did

Dexter the Great Dane. But Pixie, the little pug, refused to budge.

"Pixie, here!" Mrs Shah called again. Still the little pug didn't move. "Don't you want a treat?"

Mrs Shah walked towards Pixie, waving a doggy treat at her. But Pixie just lay down on the basketball court and closed her eyes.

Finally, Mrs Shah picked up her little dog. "I don't believe it – she's fallen asleep!"

Everyone laughed again.

"Puppies are baby dogs," said Mr Jacobs. "They like to play and they need exercise, but they also need their sleep."

Finally, it was Coco's turn. Sam stayed with Coco, while Amelia went to the other end of the basketball court.

"Coco! Here!" called Amelia.

But Coco just barked back and stayed where she was.

Amelia tried again. "Here, Coco!" She held out a doggy treat.

Suddenly, Coco charged towards Amelia. But then she saw the Great Dane and the St Bernard playing and raced off to join them, jumping up and barking at the bigger dogs.

Amelia groaned.
"Don't worry,"
said Mr Jacobs. "It
just takes practice.
Some dogs will get
the idea quicker
than others."

Just then, Amelia
spotted Tiffany
passing on the
other side of the
fence, holding a
bunch of balloons.
As usual, she
had the doggy
backpack on.

Sparkle was inside, yapping at the puppies on the basketball court.

"Hi, Tiffany," said Amelia. "Do you and Sparkle want to join our puppy training class?"

Tiffany laughed. "Sparkle doesn't need training! He's perfect the way he is."

"All puppies need training," said Sam, frowning.

"Not my Sparkle," said Tiffany. "I don't want naughty puppies teaching him bad habits. Anyway, I have to go home and get ready for my party."

As Tiffany strolled on past the basketball court, Amelia could still hear Sparkle yapping.

"I bet Sparkle would love to play with these puppies," she said, sadly.

"He must be so bored in that puppy carrier all the time," Sam agreed. "Not like Coco!" The chocolate lab was chasing Dexter and Casey around the basketball court.

Mr Jacobs took a thick piece of rope

out of a box. "Now we're going to teach the puppies how to play with toys," he said. "Time for a tug of war!"

Mr Jacobs held one end of the rope while Sherlock took the other end in his mouth. Then they both pulled. Growling and clamping his sharp teeth around the rope, the German shepherd looked quite fierce. Mr Jacobs waggled the rope around and then dropped it after a while.

"Don't let the dogs win all the time," said Mr Jacobs, "or they'll get bored of the game. And don't pull too hard as young puppies still have their baby teeth, which could get damaged."

The puppy owners each took a rope and began to play tug of war with their puppies – all except for Mrs Shah, who was still cradling her sleeping pug in her arms. Sam and Amelia took turns playing tug of war with Coco. Coco grasped the rope in her teeth. Growling, she pulled and wouldn't let go.

"I think Coco likes playing more than she likes following directions!" said Sam.

Nearby, Dexter and Casey played with each other instead of the ropes. The two big puppies rolled around on the ground, barking and yapping.

Amelia suddenly had a thought.

"Do you think one of those big dogs might have bitten Sherlock?" she asked Sam. "They're not properly trained, after all."

Sam frowned. "They seem pretty friendly to me."

Amelia nodded. "Maybe you're right." She thought of the blue ribbon they'd seen in the bushes. It was their only

clue – but she still couldn't remember
where she'd seen it before. She sighed.
"I wonder if we'll ever find the culprit?

CHAPTER FIVE

That evening, Amelia, Mum and Gran went to the Old Mill for a little party with Sam and his parents. Mr Baxter cooked jacket potatoes with a selection of toppings. Amelia piled some baked beans and cheese on to hers, with salad on the side.

For dessert, Gran had brought her famous apple pie. "I know it's your favourite, Sam," she said, winking at him.

"Mine too!" said Mr Baxter.

Amelia smiled. Ever since she and her mum had moved from the city to Gran's house in Welford, the Baxters' big old B&B had become like a second home.

In one corner of the large country-style kitchen, Mac and Coco were having a tug of war with a rubber chicken.

"Come on, Mac!" Sam cheered his little white puppy. "Pull that chicken."

But Coco wouldn't let go, pulling

and pulling until, at last, she tugged the rubber chicken away from Mac and went flying backwards across the tiled floor.

Amelia laughed. "At least Coco learned *something* at puppy training class today."

Suddenly, they heard a loud screech. Then came a *BOOM!* The two puppies shot under the kitchen table.

Through the window, Amelia saw a shower of glittering sparks in the night sky. "I guess Tiffany's fireworks have started," she said.

Another rocket screeched up into the air and burst with a loud bang. Under the table, Mac and Coco yelped.

"Why don't you two take Mac and Coco upstairs?" said Mrs Baxter. "Try to keep them calm."

Amelia and Sam crawled under the table and pulled out the frightened puppies. As Amelia followed Sam and Mac up the stairs, cuddling Coco, more rockets went off and the puppy nearly squirmed out of her grasp.

"It's OK, Coco," she said softly. "Don't worry."

"Poor little scaredy-dogs!" said Sam, ruffling Mac's ears.

They carried the puppies to an empty guest room. The moment they set the

dogs down, Coco and Mac scampered
under the bed to hide.

"Let's make a cosy den for them," said
Amelia. "Mr Hope said that should help
them feel safe."

There wasn't much space under
the bed, but they tried to make it
comfortable with some blankets and
cushions. The puppies huddled together

under a blanket. Every time they heard another rocket go off, the puppies whimpered and their tails quivered.

"Those are really amazing fireworks," said Amelia, peering out the window. "I just wish they weren't so close by!"

"Tiffany lives on the lane right behind

us," said Sam. He pointed out of the window. "That's her house."

Sam pulled a bag of dog treats from

his pocket. He handed some to Amelia and they fed the treats to Mac and Coco. Another rocket exploded outside, but the puppies were too busy with their treats to notice.

"I think they're calm now," said Amelia. "Let's go back downstairs."

But halfway down, Amelia stopped. "Do you hear that whining and scratching?" she asked Sam.

Sam nodded. "It's not Coco or Mac, though. It sounds like it's coming from outside."

Together, they rushed to the back door. As Sam pulled it open, a little ball of white fur dashed inside.

"Sparkle!" Amelia gasped. "What are you doing here?"

Tiffany's puppy hid behind the welly boots lined up near the door. Another rocket screeched and boomed outside, and Sparkle yelped in fear.

Amelia reached forwards to pick up the puppy. She could feel his body trembling. "Sparkle must be afraid of the fireworks too!" she said. "Maybe we should bring him upstairs to the den. We can take him back to Tiffany's house when the fireworks are over."

In the guest room, Mac and Coco peeked out from under the bed.

"Hello, you two," said Sam, giving

them each a
stroke. "We've
brought you a
friend."

Amelia set
Sparkle on the
carpet and Mac trotted over, followed
by Coco. But as the other puppies
approached, Sparkle bared his teeth and
snarled at them.

"I've never seen him do that before!"
said Sam.

Amelia frowned. "Be nice, Sparkle,"
she said. "Mac and Coco just want to be
friends with you."

More fireworks screeched and

boomed. Suddenly, Sparkle leapt on Coco, and with another loud snarl, the puppy sank his teeth into Coco's back leg. Coco yelped in pain.

"No!" yelled Amelia, as Coco scrambled back under the bed. Amelia grabbed Sparkle's collar and dragged him away from the other puppies.

Meanwhile, Sam squeezed under the bed to check on Coco. "Are you OK?" he said anxiously.

"What's all the noise?" asked Mr Ferguson from the doorway.

He noticed Amelia holding Sparkle by the collar. "Another dog? Is this a B&B or an animal shelter?"

As Mr Ferguson skulked off, Mrs Baxter came up the stairs with Amelia's mum, her gran and Mr Baxter. All of them looked confused.

"We let Sparkle in through the back door," Amelia told them, speaking quickly. Her heart was beating wildly. "He was scared of the fireworks, so we brought him up here."

Sam crawled back out from under the bed with Coco, a worried look on his face. One of the puppy's back legs was bleeding.

"Sparkle bit Coco," he said.

"Oh no," said Mrs Baxter. "It looks like we need another trip to Animal Ark. I'll ring the Hopes and ask if they can open the surgery."

"I'll ring Tiffany's parents, and tell them where Sparkle is," said Mr Baxter.

Amelia and Sam followed Mrs Baxter downstairs, carrying Coco, and climbed into the car.

"Poor Coco." Amelia stroked the puppy's chocolate-brown fur.

"First Sherlock gets bitten, and now Coco …" said Sam. "Don't you think that's a weird coincidence?"

Amelia looked over at him in the dark

car. She suddenly remembered the blue ribbon she'd seen in the bush outside Mr Jacobs's house – and knew now why it looked familiar. *Sparkle usually wears a blue bow!*

"Sam ..." said Amelia. "What if Sparkle is the dog who bit Sherlock?"

CHAPTER SIX

When they arrived at Animal Ark, the lights were off, but Mrs Hope was on the step, unlocking the door. "Has the bleeding got worse?" she asked, as she led them inside.

Amelia shook her head. In the consulting room, Sam put Coco on the examining table. The little puppy continued to whimper and whine, licking her lips nervously.

"Are you sure it was Sparkle who bit her?" Mrs Hope asked.

Amelia and Sam both nodded, gently stroking Coco to keep her still while Mrs Hope examined her leg. "We saw it," added Amelia.

Mrs Hope shaved off some of Coco's blood-stained fur, so she could clean the wound. She dabbed away the dried blood with a cotton pad and hydrogen peroxide. Amelia saw two small puncture marks where Sparkle's teeth had gone into Coco's skin.

"Luckily, the wound isn't serious," said Mrs Hope. "It will heal quicker if it's left open without a bandage over it. But you'll have to clean it."

"Twice a day?" said Amelia.

"With a cotton pad and salt water?" said Sam.

Mrs Hope looked impressed. "I can see you've been learning a lot here!"

Amelia exchanged a smile with Sam.

Mrs Hope fetched a clear plastic cone that looked a bit like a lampshade and fitted the narrower end over Coco's neck. The wider end of the cone went around the

puppy's head so she couldn't reach her injury.

"We don't want Coco to bite or scratch her wound," said Mrs Hope. "Otherwise it could get infected."

Coco pawed at the cone and tried to pull it off. When she realised it wouldn't come off, she began to whine.

"I'm sorry, Coco," said Sam, rubbing her nose. "But it's for your own good."

Amelia felt a flush of anger at seeing the sad puppy. "She was just trying to be friendly to Sparkle. Tiffany's got to train her dog to behave better!"

Sam nodded. "But how are we going to convince her?"

They arrived back at the Old Mill
to find Tiffany and her father on the
doorstep.

Tiffany was scowling. "Your dad
phoned to say that Sparkle's here," she
said to Sam. "What's the deal?"

"Sparkle's inside," said Sam. He was
carrying Coco in his arms. "But look –
he bit Coco."

Tiffany shook her head angrily.
"I don't believe that my little Sparkle
Barkle did that."

"Your little Sparkle Barkle *did* do
that," said Amelia, hands on her hips.
"We saw him. He came here because

he was frightened of the fireworks, and then he bit Coco."

Tiffany turned red. Her dad's face was grim.

Mrs Baxter opened the door. "Let's talk about it inside," she said.

Tiffany pushed her way into the house. "Sparkle Barkle!" she called. "Where are you?"

Mr Baxter greeted everyone and took Coco from Sam. "Sparkle's in the living room," he said. "I'll take Coco upstairs. I think Mac is missing her."

In the living room, they couldn't see Sparkle at first. Then Amelia spotted him hiding under an armchair.

"Sparkle Barkle, I'm here!" said Tiffany, reaching under the chair for her fluffy white puppy.

Growling, Sparkle shrank further back, out of reach.

"Why are you growling at me?" asked Tiffany.

"He was really frightened by the fireworks," said Amelia. "I'd be careful if I were you."

"You should have seen how he was panicking while those rockets were going off," said Sam.

Mr Banks sighed. "We should have known better. Tiff really wanted fireworks on her birthday. We didn't think about how they might affect Sparkle."

Amelia bit her tongue to stop herself from blurting what she was thinking – *We tried to tell her but she wouldn't listen!*

Tiffany reached back under the chair for the little puppy, but he growled at her again.

"Sparkle, don't do that." Tiffany frowned and stood up. "I thought he'd love the fireworks! I even brought him outside to watch with me, but that's when he ran off."

"And bit poor Coco!" said Sam.

That reminded Amelia. "Tiffany, do you ever walk Sparkle down the road from the village shop? You know, near Scarecrow Cottage?"

Tiffany narrowed her eyes. "Sometimes. I let him out of his backpack so that he can run around in the bushes and have a wee. So what?"

"We found a blue ribbon in the bushes," said Amelia.

"I wondered where that went!" cried Tiffany. "Sparkle lost it yesterday."

"I think he also bit Sherlock, Mr Jacobs's German shepherd," said Amelia. "Maybe he was scared because Sherlock's so big. He was at Animal Ark yesterday, getting his bite treated."

"Sparkle was probably just playing," muttered Tiffany. "As if he could hurt a big dog like that." She leaned down, reaching under the chair again to pick up her puppy, but he snapped at her.

"Sparkle!" she cried, snatching her hand back. "Naughty!"

"He's just scared!" said Amelia.

Tiffany scowled. Tears welled up in her eyes.

"Come on, Tiff," said Mr Banks. "Let's

take Sparkle home and get back to your party."

"Here." Sam pulled some dog treats out of his pocket and gave them to Mr Banks. "See if these will coax him out."

At last, the little puppy crawled out from under the chair. Tiffany picked him up carefully and put him in the doggy backpack, but Sparkle squirmed and peered out sadly through the mesh.

"Thank you for looking after Sparkle," said Mr Banks. He gave his daughter a meaningful look. Tiffany stared back at him, a little disgruntled, until she finally gave a huff.

"Would you like to come over for

some of my birthday cake?" she said. "I suppose you did look after Sparkle."

"That would be lovely," said Mr Baxter.

As soon as they arrived at the Bankses' house, Tiffany's mother settled Sparkle down in the kitchen on his doggy bed.

"You be a good dog tomorrow," Tiffany told him. "No more biting!"

They all gathered around a table on the patio of the Bankses' garden with the rest of Tiffany's party guests, while Coco and Mac chased each other around on the lawn. Fairy lights decorated the trees and candles flickered on the cake, which was almost as big as Sparkle.

Tiffany stood behind the cake as everyone sang "Happy Birthday".

"Make a wish!" cried Mrs Banks as Tiffany blew out the candles.

I hope Tiffany wished for Sparkle to stop biting, thought Amelia as Mr Banks passed round slices of cake. Coco and Mac trotted over to the table when they saw the cake being served.

"None for you, Coco," said Sam, laughing.

The puppies went back to playing, ducking under the table and back out again, their tails wagging.

The dogs are much happier now the fireworks are over, Amelia thought. Coco didn't even seem to mind the cone too much any more.

Amelia took a bite of birthday cake, then looked back towards the house, where Sparkle lay in his doggy bed. *Poor*

Sparkle, Amelia thought. He was missing out on all the fun. Mr Hope had said that dogs only bit other dogs when they were scared. Sparkle wasn't a bad dog – he was just a scaredy-dog!

We've got to convince Tiffany to take Sparkle to training classes! thought Amelia. Being around other dogs would help Sparkle not to be afraid of them. She was sure that Sparkle could learn to be a good dog, if only his owner would agree to it …

STORY TWO:
PUPPY HERO

CHAPTER ONE

The next morning, Amelia and Sam
brought Coco to dog training class.
The big cone around the puppy's neck
didn't stop her from bounding around
the basketball court with the other dogs.
The spring sun shone in a cloudless blue
sky and a sparrow chirped from the top

of the tall metal fence that surrounded the court.

"Today, we're going to practise walking the puppies on their leads," said Mr Jacobs. "Sherlock and I will demonstrate." Unlike the lively puppies, the German shepherd stood obediently beside his owner, waiting for instructions. "When out walking, always keep your puppy on the same side. Use the word 'heel' when they're walking correctly so they learn what it means."

Mr Jacobs started to walk. "Sherlock, heel," he said. The German shepherd walked alongside him. "You don't want your puppy to get ahead of you and pull you along. If they do get ahead of you, either stop or change direction." Mr Jacobs turned slightly so Sherlock's nose was roughly even with him. "Eventually they'll get the message. Right, Sherlock?"

He stopped, and Sherlock immediately stopped too. "Good dog." Mr Jacobs leaned over and stroked Sherlock's head. "Is everyone ready to give it a try?"

But before they had a chance, the gate into the basketball court opened and Mr and Mrs Banks came in. Tiffany, who was wearing her doggy backpack, followed behind them.

Has she come to join the puppy training

classes after all? Amelia wondered.

"Tiffany looks even grumpier than usual," Sam whispered.

Sam was right. Tiffany's arms were crossed in front of her and her brows were drawn together in an angry scowl.

"Have you got something to say to Mr Jacobs?" prompted her mother.

Tiffany looked down at the ground.
"Um …" Tiffany stammered. "I'm sorry.
I think it might have been Sparkle who
bit your dog."

"Thank you for apologising," said Mr
Jacobs. "Dogs can get out of hand if
they're not trained properly. Would you
and Sparkle like to join our classes?"

"No, I—" Tiffany began.

"That would be marvellous!"
interrupted Mrs Banks. "Don't you
remember, Tiffany? Mr and Mrs Hope
recommended puppy training classes."

"We took Sparkle to Animal
Ark earlier to ask advice about his
behaviour," Mr Banks explained.

"The Hopes also recommended something else," Tiffany's mother added. "Tiff, do you want to show Mr Jacobs?"

Tiffany gave a heavy sigh and took Sparkle out of the backpack. A muzzle covered the puppy's mouth.

Tiffany huffed. "This makes him look so ugly."

Sparkle doesn't look happy, thought Amelia. The little dog's expression seemed to match Tiffany's scowl.

"It's just temporary," said Mr Banks. "Until he learns not to bite."

Mr Jacobs looked sympathetic. "Sparkle bites because he's anxious and afraid of other dogs. He needs to feel comfortable with them, and with people too. We were just about to practise walking the puppies on their leads. Why don't you join us?"

"But I can just carry Sparkle in his backpack," said Tiffany.

"Dogs need exercise," said Mr Jacobs. "They need to walk and run and play, just like children do. If they don't get enough activity, their energy has nowhere to go, so they start acting out."

Amelia glanced at Sam. "That would definitely explain why Sparkle has been biting lately," she murmured.

Sam nodded. "And why he ran off."

"Dogs also need a chance to use their noses," said Mr Jacobs.

"Their noses?" said Amelia.

Mr Jacobs nodded. "They need to be able to smell things around them. If Sparkle is carried in the doggy backpack all the time, he won't get used to the smell of things on the ground. New dog scents might seem dangerous to him."

"I didn't know that!" said Mr Banks. "Listen to Mr Jacobs, Tiffany. He's the expert."

Tiffany rolled her eyes, but she clipped

on Sparkle's lead and set him down on the ground next to her.

"Excellent," said Mr Jacobs. "Okay, how about if Coco tries walking on the lead first?"

Sam gave Amelia the lead. "You have a go," he said.

But just as Amelia began to walk with Coco, one of the sparrows on the fence flew down on to the basketball court. The puppy took off at once.

"Coco, slow down!" Amelia held tightly to the lead as the little brown puppy pulled her along. The sparrow flitted away, but Coco kept running, tugging Amelia along with her.

"You're supposed to walk behind me, not run in front!" called Amelia.

Coco dragged Amelia across the basketball court towards the other puppies. She barked at Sparkle and ran in circles around him.

"Stop that!" said Tiffany. "Your silly puppy is tangling up the leads!"

Sparkle barked back and jumped up

and down excitedly.

"Sorry," said Amelia, panting.

"We'll sort it out," said Sam, running over to help.

Just then, Coco rolled over on to her back with her tummy up.

"Well done, Coco," said Mr Jacobs. "That's good playing behaviour! Showing her tummy means that she

wants to be friends."

Sparkle kept barking at Coco, standing over her while Coco was still showing her tummy.

Mr Jacobs frowned. "Hmm … Sparkle should have rolled over too. Instead, he tried to show that he was in charge. Sparkle has to learn how to play nicely."

"Maybe he just doesn't want to be friends with Coco," said Tiffany. She scooped up Sparkle and stormed off.

"I think Tiffany needs to learn how to play nicely too," Amelia whispered.

"You're right," said Sam. "Too bad there aren't any training classes for stroppy dog-owners!"

CHAPTER TWO

The next day, Coco trotted obediently alongside Amelia, her brown head poking out from the plastic cone. The class was taking a stroll around Welford to practise walking the puppies on leads. As the group passed the duck pond, Coco briefly looked in the direction of the three ducks swimming lazily up and down, but she didn't try to run towards them, as Amelia expected her to.

"Well done, Coco!" she said, leaning down to stroke the puppy.

Mr Jacobs was at the front of the group with Sherlock. The German shepherd still had his bandage on, but it didn't seem to bother him. Sam had brought Mac along for the walk too. Behind them were Dexter and Casey

with their owners. Mr Fanelli followed
with JJ, who tried to run off every which
way. Mrs Shah had to cajole Pixie to
keep up with the others, as the little pug
wanted to play with two girls kicking a
football on the grass.

"Sparkle, stop it!" Amelia heard
behind her. She turned to see Tiffany
pulling her puppy out of a pile of grass
cuttings. Sparkle wore his muzzle, a new
blue bow on his head, and a sparkly

new collar. "You're so mucky, Sparkle Barkle. Honestly, you never get this dirty when you're in your backpack."

Suddenly, Sparkle gave an excited yap and tugged hard on his lead. He raced across the park, dragging Tiffany towards a nearby house, where a young woman with curly dark hair was washing her car in the drive.

"Sparkle, stop!" Tiffany called.

Sparkle paid no attention. He ran towards the bucket of water, which was on the ground next to the car. The woman smiled at him. Yapping playfully, Sparkle leapt up on his hind legs and knocked the bucket over with his front

paws. Soapy water sloshed all over the
drive. The puppy started splashing about
in the puddle, flicking the water around
with his paws.

The woman laughed. "You're a
mischievous pup, aren't you?" she said to
Sparkle.

Amelia suddenly felt Coco's lead fly

out of her hand. The little brown puppy dashed towards the water.

"Coco, stop!" she called.

Amelia ran after Coco, followed by Sam and Mac. They caught up with the chocolate Labrador just as she was trying to climb into the bucket. But the cone around her head got in her way.

Amelia picked up the squirming puppy. "Coco! You're going to get your wound wet!"

Tiffany gingerly plucked a wet Sparkle out of the water. His usually fluffy white fur was soaked and stuck down flat to his little body. She held him out in front of her, but he shook the water off. Drops went flying, drenching Tiffany.

"You naughty dog, Sparkle!" spluttered Tiffany. "Everything's wet, even your pretty bow. And now you've got me wet too!"

Amelia laughed. "Dogs really love playing in water, don't they?"

Tiffany glared at her.

Mr Jacobs and the rest of the class were finally catching up. Sherlock walked obediently behind his owner.

Amelia felt her heart sinking. *Coco and Sparkle will never be as well behaved as Sherlock!*

"I'm sorry, Mr Jacobs," said Amelia. "The puppies just ran off."

Mr Jacobs leaned over and ruffled Sparkle's wet ears. "Well I must say, I'm glad to see him looking so happy."

But Sparkle's owner didn't look at all happy.

"Sparkle learns quickly," said Mr Jacobs. "If you come back to classes, he'll soon be well trained."

"He *is* a clever dog," said Tiffany. "And he doesn't need any classes."

As soon as Mr Jacobs turned his back, Amelia saw Tiffany put Sparkle back in his backpack. He stared out sadly through the mesh.

I guess Tiffany's not coming back to class, thought Amelia. *Poor Sparkle!*

CHAPTER THREE

That afternoon, Amelia and Sam took
Coco to Animal Ark so that Mrs Hope
could check her bite wound. Amelia was
happy to see that the tooth marks had
scabbed over.

"It's healing nicely," said Mrs Hope.
"But we'll leave the cone on a little

longer, just to be on the safe side."

Mr Hope peered around the door. "Would you two like to stay and help with my next patient?" he asked Amelia and Sam.

"Sure!" said Amelia. "But what should we do with Coco?"

"She can help, too," said Mr Hope. "The patient is a puppy who needs to practise being around other dogs. Stay right here. I'll bring him in."

Sam raised an eyebrow at Amelia. "I bet I know who it is …"

Sure enough, Mr Hope returned with Tiffany and Sparkle, still in his backpack. Tiffany had changed out of her wet clothes, but she was still wearing her scowl.

"Not you two again," she huffed. "And that naughty puppy, too."

Amelia bit her lip to stop herself from replying. Luckily, Coco sat patiently between her and Sam.

Tiffany took Sparkle out of the backpack and set him on the examining

table. The little puppy still had the muzzle over his mouth.

"Sparkle keeps scratching," Tiffany told Mr Hope. "He must have caught fleas from one of the dogs at puppy training class." She shot a glance at Coco. "It was probably her."

"Coco doesn't have fleas!" said Sam.

Mr Hope checked Sparkle's fur under a bright light. He separated tufts of hair to look at Sparkle's skin, then gave the puppy's fur a rub. Amelia checked the examination table to see if any flea droppings had fallen out. She couldn't see a thing.

"No sign of fleas," Mr Hope said at

last. "If you give Sparkle a monthly treatment, it shouldn't be an issue. My guess is that Sparkle scratches himself because he's bored."

Tiffany wrinkled her nose. "But I take him out in his backpack every day."

"Wouldn't you be bored riding in a backpack all the time, without having a chance to walk around in the fresh air and play?" Mr Hope asked her.

"Sparkle hates getting his paws dirty," said Tiffany.

"But he needs exercise," said Mr Hope.

Tiffany hesitated. She looked as though she might be about to cry, and Amelia suddenly felt sorry for her. "I just wanted him to feel safe," said Tiffany.

"I'm afraid the backpack is doing just the opposite," said Mr Hope. "Dogs need to be active, and they love exploring the world around them. If Sparkle's life was a bit more interesting, I'm sure he'd stop scratching."

"Can we take the muzzle off?" asked Tiffany.

"Not yet, I'm afraid," said Mr Hope. "Not until he learns not to bite." He smiled kindly. "Sparkle's not a bad dog, Tiffany. He just needs to be taught good behaviour."

Tiffany nodded. "Thank you," she mumbled. She put on Sparkle's lead.

Then she gently lifted him off the table and walked him out of the consulting room. Amelia and Sam followed with Coco.

In the reception area, Tiffany sat on a chair and cuddled Sparkle on her lap. When she looked up, Amelia could see tears streaking down her cheeks.

"Oh, Sparkle Barkle," whispered Tiffany, stroking the puppy, "I promise that I'll try harder from now on."

Tiffany really does love her dog, thought Amelia.

She sat in the seat next to Tiffany. "Would you let us help?" she asked.

Tiffany sniffled. "How?"

"For starters, we could help you train him," said Sam. "Mr Jacobs says that a well-trained dog is a happy dog."

"Sparkle can practise training with Coco," said Amelia. She patted the little brown Labrador. "You really want to be friends with Sparkle, don't you, Coco?"

Coco wagged her tail.

"What do you say?" Sam asked Tiffany.

Tiffany hesitated for a moment. "OK,"

she said, kissing the top of Sparkle's head. "I'll do anything for Sparkle."

Amelia grinned. "Come on," she said. "Let's get started!"

CHAPTER FOUR

Before long, they were in the garden at the Old Mill. Amelia and Sam giggled as the three puppies rolled on to their backs to show their tummies. Coco was having a bit of trouble rolling with the plastic cone around her neck.

"Sparkle will get all dirty rolling

around like that," said Tiffany, frowning.

Sparkle scrambled up and bowed
to the other puppies, his front paws
stretched out and his bottom in the air.

"He's happy," said Amelia, pointing.
"Look how his tail is wagging!"

"I thought we were supposed to be
training him," grumbled Tiffany.

"OK, let's practise recall first," said
Sam. "Mac!" he called. "Here, Mac."

The Westie puppy perked up his ears and trotted across the lawn towards him.

Sam patted his head. "Good boy."

Next it was Coco's turn. "Coco!" called Amelia, from the bottom of the garden. "Here, Coco."

Coco carried on rolling around on the grass. Amelia tried again. "Coco! Here, Coco!" At last, the puppy stopped rolling and scampered towards her. "Well done!" Amelia ruffled the puppy's ears.

Then it was Tiffany's turn. "Sparkle! Here, Sparkle!" But instead of coming, Sparkle trotted over to the flower beds to sniff the tulips. "Come on, boy," Tiffany called again. Sparkle sat down

on the grass. Tiffany threw up her
hands. "It's no use."

"Keep trying," urged Amelia. "He'll
learn eventually."

"Try using a toy," suggested Sam. He
threw Mac's rubber chicken to Tiffany.

Holding the toy out so Sparkle could
see it, Tiffany called, "Sparkle, come!"

At last, the little dog trotted down
to the bottom of the garden. Tiffany
grinned. "Good dog, Sparkle Barkle,"
she said, stroking his fluffy fur.

They practised some more, and soon
all of the puppies came when they were
called.

"Mr Jacobs will be impressed," said

Sam, with a grin. "Sparkle's getting the hang of it!"

"I knew he was a clever dog," said Tiffany proudly.

"Shall we practise walking on the lead now?" asked Amelia.

"Let's take the puppies across the fields," said Sam. "Tiffany, you can borrow a pair of wellies."

With their wellies on, they set off down a path at the edge of the fields, the three puppies wagging their tails. The sun shone from between the clouds and neat rows of green shoots poked up from the fine brown soil in the fields. Mac walked obediently behind Sam, but Coco and Sparkle both pulled at their leads, wanting to dash off and explore. Every so often, Amelia and Tiffany stopped so the puppies learned to walk at their pace.

I can't believe I'm actually having fun hanging out with Tiffany, thought Amelia, smiling to herself.

They were in a meadow of long grass

and wildflowers when Amelia noticed that the sun had disappeared behind the grey clouds. A gust of wind made her shiver. She turned to the others. "We should probably head—"

Amelia winced as a flash of lightning startled all three of them. A few seconds later, a rumble of thunder rolled over their heads, as fat drops of rain began to fall.

"Whoa!" said Amelia.

"Let's go and shelter over there!" called Sam, pointing to a grove of trees on the edge of the meadow. They pulled their hoods up and ran beneath the branches. Thunder growled across the

meadow. The three puppies huddled
together, trembling.

"Oh no!" said Amelia. "It's like the
fireworks all over again."

Another crack of thunder sounded,
making Amelia jump. She could feel her
heart thumping in her chest. *It's OK*, she
told herself, trying to take deep, calming
breaths. Beside her, Sparkle was huddled
against Coco, panting, his eyes wide. *It*

must be even worse for the puppies, thought Amelia. *They don't understand what thunder is!*

"That's it," said Tiffany. "I'm going back to using Sparkle's backpack."

"But he doesn't like it in there," said Amelia.

"Mr and Mrs Hope said it's not good for him," said Sam.

Tiffany ignored them. She reached down to pick up the little puppy, but Sparkle wriggled out of her hands. Amelia watched in horror as he darted off through the trees.

"Sparkle!" called Tiffany, but her voice was drowned out by a clap of thunder.

She chased after the puppy. Holding Mac and Coco's leads tightly, Amelia and Sam ran after her.

"Where's he gone?" said Amelia. She could see trees and bushes and the meadow beyond, but she couldn't see the little white puppy anywhere.

"Call him, Tiffany," Sam suggested. "He knows how to do recall now."

"Sparkle! Here, Sparkle!" Tiffany shouted, her eyes wide with desperation.

They waited, but Sparkle didn't come.

"Sparkle! Here, boy!" Tiffany tried again.

They moved on through the grove of trees. Tiffany kept calling for Sparkle as they searched the meadow for a flash of white fur but there was still no sign of him. *Where's he got to?* wondered Amelia.

Amelia's hoodie was no protection from the pouring rain, and she was wet through. She felt the rain drip off her hair and trickle down her back. Sam and Tiffany were soaked as well. Every so often, another rumble of thunder made Mac and Coco shudder. The puppies' wet fur clung to their bodies.

Coco tugged at her lead. "Coco,

sit," said Amelia. But Coco pulled harder, her body straining against the collar.

"We don't want you to get lost too, Coco," said Sam.

Suddenly, Amelia had an idea. "I wonder if Coco can find Sparkle? After all, if dogs like Sherlock can track down criminals, maybe Coco can find Sparkle."

Tiffany's face brightened. "Let's give it a try."

"But I promised Auntie Jen I would look after Coco properly," said Sam, looking anxious. "I can't let anything happen to her."

"Oh, please! Sparkle will be so frightened by the storm!" said Tiffany. "We've got to find him."

Coco was tugging the lead so hard now that Amelia struggled to keep hold of it. "I have a hunch that Coco can help," said Amelia. "Besides, she can do recall really well now. She'll come back when we call her."

Sam was frowning, but he nodded. "OK."

Amelia unclipped the lead from Coco's collar. The little puppy dashed off through the trees. But then she stopped and turned around.

Amelia felt a flicker of hope. "I think

she wants us to follow her!"

Coco ran across the meadow and down a slope. Amelia, Tiffany and Sam followed with Mac. They came to a stream at the bottom. Amelia could see Coco standing on the bank, gazing across the water and barking. Amelia ran to her, half sliding in the mud. When she reached the bottom, she saw what Coco was barking at.

On a little island in the middle of the stream was the bedraggled white puppy. As Amelia got nearer, she saw that the island was actually just a log that had got lodged against some stones in the water. Sparkle stood on the log, wet

and shivering. But when he saw Coco and the others on the bank, he began to bark.

"Sparkle!" called Tiffany.

"He must have fallen in the stream and been swept out by the current," said Sam. "Well done, Coco. You found him!"

But Amelia felt worried. *We've found Sparkle, but we might be about to lose him again … for good!* The water was surging fast, jiggling the log against the stones. If Sparkle fell in, he would be carried downstream. They needed to get Sparkle to safety – and fast!

CHAPTER FIVE

"Can we go and get him?" Tiffany asked.

Sam shook his head. "It's too dangerous. We might slip if we go in …"

"And it's too far for one person to reach Sparkle from the bank," said Amelia. She gasped as she had a

brainwave. "But three people might
have a chance!"

"What do you mean?" asked Sam.

"Let's make a chain to reach Sparkle,"
said Amelia. "Sam, you stand here
on the bank and hold Tiffany's hand.
Tiffany, I'll take your other hand, then
you and I will wade into the water as
far as we can."

Sam took off his jacket and put it

over Mac and Coco. "The puppies can shelter from the storm under here," he said.

They held hands and formed a line out to the log – first Sam, then Tiffany, and finally Amelia. She shivered as the cold water came over the top of her wellies and filled up her boots. The heavy rain slapping against the stream was so loud she could barely

hear Sam asking if she was steady. With one hand, she clung tightly to Tiffany. With the other, she reached out to Sparkle, who was whining and wriggling on the log. *Nearly there …*

A roar of thunder sounded overhead, startling Sparkle, who almost fell off the log. Amelia's heart was in her mouth as she watched the little dog find his footing again. She stretched her hand out until the tips of her fingers brushed the edge of the log. But she couldn't quite reach Sparkle.

"Come on, Sparkle," she coaxed the puppy. He was jerking his body as if he wanted to jump, but staying fixed in place. Then Amelia saw why.

"Oh no!" she called to the others over the rush of water. "Sparkle's bow is caught on the log!"

"Is he hurt?" asked Tiffany.

"No, but I can't reach him," said Amelia. "We need to get closer."

Sam inched along until he had one foot on the bank and the other in the water.

Tiffany stretched her arms wide. "Can you reach him now?" she asked, her voice shaking. "I can't stretch any further!"

Amelia leaned towards Sparkle again, reaching out her free hand as far as it would go. Her fingers caught the end of Sparkle's bow. She tugged it and the bow fell from the twig it had been caught on. *Yes!* The bow floated downstream as Sparkle barked and shook his head.

Relief rushed through Amelia.

"Come on, Sparkle," called Tiffany.

Sparkle wagged his tail and barked at his owner. Then suddenly, he leapt off the log towards her … and missed. He landed in the water, his little white head bobbing above the water as the current swept him downstream.

"Sparkle!" shrieked Tiffany.

Amelia spotted Sparkle's lead trailing

behind him in the water. She made a grab for it with her free hand, but it floated just past her grasp. She snatched for it again, pulling Tiffany and Sam along with her – and this time, she managed to hang on to it.

"I've got him!" she called.

Still holding hands, they waded back to the bank. Amelia clung to Sparkle's lead, pulling him through the water behind her, until at last he scrambled up on to the bank and jumped into

Tiffany's open arms.

"Oh, my little Sparkle
Barkle," crooned Tiffany,
as she cradled Sparkle
against her chest. "I'm so
glad you're safe."

The puppy's muddy paws were
making Tiffany's pink top dirty, but
for once, she didn't complain. She just
laughed. "You are definitely going
straight in the bath when we get home."

"We're lucky the water was shallow,"
said Amelia.

Sam nodded vigorously. "If it had
been any deeper, it would have been too
dangerous to go in." He glanced up at

the sky. "Hey, the thunder's stopped."

"So has the rain," said Amelia. She looked up at the sky and saw a shaft of sunlight streaming through the clouds. *We did it!* she thought. *We saved Sparkle.*

Amelia pulled her wellies off, one at a time, to pour the water back into the river. Sam knelt down to take his sodden jacket from Mac and Coco. The two puppies leapt up, knocking him backwards. When Sam got up, Amelia saw that there was mud covering the back of his jeans. "I think we'll all need a bath," she said, smiling.

Drips of water trickled down Tiffany's face and on to Sparkle, who was still

nestled in her arms. Amelia wasn't sure
if they were raindrops or teardrops.

Tiffany took a deep breath. "Thank
you," she said to Amelia and Sam. "I
was so scared I would lose Sparkle. But
you two helped me rescue him."

"Don't forget Coco," said Amelia. "It
was Coco who found Sparkle."

Tiffany stroked Coco's wet fur.
"Thank you, Coco," she said. "You're a
hero."

"She is, isn't she?" said Sam. "Just wait till Auntie Jen hears about this!"

The three of them laughed as they started walking away from the stream, their wellies squelching in the grass.

"Hey, look," said Tiffany. She pointed to the sky, where a shimmering arc had emerged from the clouds. "A rainbow!"

Amelia grinned up at the rainbow. "It's beautiful," she said.

"It almost makes the storm worth it!" said Sam.

As they walked the puppies home, Amelia's heart was filled with hope – and not just because of the rainbow. Tiffany had come close to losing Sparkle today. Now hopefully she understood how important it was to be a responsible dog owner.

CHAPTER SIX

"I can't believe it's the last class!" Sam said to Amelia. "Coco's learned so much."

It was the end of the week, and they were at the basketball court for the final time. Coco was playing with the big puppies – Dexter and Casey. They took turns rolling over and showing their tummies, although Coco was still having a bit of trouble with the big plastic cone around her neck.

As Amelia watched the puppies play, Dexter swatted at Casey with his big paw. Casey barked and jumped up on to him, his mouth around Dexter's neck.

Amelia gasped. "Casey's not hurting Dexter, is he?"

"No, it's just a play bite," said Mr Jacobs, smiling. "Casey's not using his teeth. Actually, it shows that the dogs are comfortable with each other."

On the other side of the basketball court, Mrs Shah's pug, Pixie, played

tug-of-war with JJ, the dachshund. Sherlock stood tall, his tail wagging as he watched over all the puppies like a proud teacher.

Mr Jacobs had brought party food to celebrate the end of the classes. Amelia and Sam chatted to him as they drank orange juice and ate biscuits. Mr Jacobs had brought healthy dog treats for the puppies, too.

"I wonder where Tiffany and Sparkle are?" said Sam.

"I hope they don't miss class," said Mr Jacobs.

"Here we are!" said Tiffany, coming through the gate behind them. "Sparkle Barkle wouldn't want to miss the last class."

Amelia could hardly believe it – Sparkle was walking on his lead just behind Tiffany, his tail wagging happily despite the muzzle over his mouth.

Mr Jacobs' face broke into a wide grin. "I see you and Sparkle have been practising walking on the lead. He's really got the idea now. Well done!"

"Where's your doggy backpack?" Amelia asked.

Tiffany shrugged. "I threw it away." She crouched down to stroke her fluffy little puppy. "Sparkle and I don't need it any more."

Mr Jacobs handed her a cup of orange juice and a biscuit. "That's the spirit! I'll bet Sparkle is much happier walking along with you."

Suddenly, Amelia noticed something else that was different about Sparkle. "He's not wearing a bow on his head!" she said.

"Well, I don't want him getting stuck again, do I?" said Tiffany.

Amelia and Sam looked at each other and grinned.

I can't believe how much Tiffany's learned this week! thought Amelia.

"Plus, I think my Sparkle Barkle looks even prettier without a bow," said Tiffany. "Well, apart from that ugly muzzle."

Tiffany took off Sparkle's lead and he joined the other puppies. Mr Jacobs brought out a bunch of balls, rubber bones, squeaky toys and teething toys for them to play with.

Sparkle rolled over and showed his tummy. Then he bowed to Coco, lowering his front legs to the ground and raising his bottom in the air.

"Sparkle's showing Coco that they're

friends," said
Mr Jacobs.
"He's playing
really well

with the other dogs now. He's not trying
to be the boss any more."

"My Sparkle Barkle is such a good
little puppy!" said Tiffany proudly.

Sparkle joined Coco in chasing a
ball. Then he rolled over and bowed to
Casey. They bounded about together,
while Coco and Pixie took turns
tugging on a rubber ring. The puppies
kept changing their playing partners.

As Sparkle approached another puppy,
Mr Jacobs turned to Tiffany. "It doesn't

look like he needs that muzzle any more."

Tiffany's eyes grew wide. "You don't think he'll bite again, do you?" she asked.

"I'm sure of it," said Mr Jacobs. "He doesn't see the other dogs as a threat now."

They watched as Sparkle and Casey chased each other around the basketball court, barking happily. When Sparkle stopped for a rest, Mr Jacobs went over and quickly pulled the muzzle strap over the puppy's head to slip it off. Sparkle looked up for a moment, confused. Then he ran off after the bigger dog and jumped on him, his mouth open.

Amelia gasped, worried that Sparkle would bite. But then Sparkle leapt down to the ground and rolled over on to his back. Casey licked him.

"They're just playing!" said Mr Jacobs.

"Well done, Sparkle!" called Tiffany.

Tail wagging, Sparkle danced around in celebration. Sherlock trotted over and nuzzled the little puppy proudly.

"Sherlock thinks that Sparkle's done well, too," said Amelia.

"All of the puppies have," said Mr Jacobs. He put his cup down and spoke up. "Can I have your attention, everyone? I'd like to thank you all for bringing your puppies to these classes. You've all worked very hard to train your dogs. So now I've got something special for you. Would you all call your puppies, please?"

"I wonder what it is?" said Sam.

"We'll soon find out," said Amelia. "Coco!" she called. "Here, Coco!"

The little brown puppy came racing across the basketball court to sit at Amelia's side. "Well done!" she whispered, ruffling Coco's ears.

"Coco, you and your trainers can be first." Mr Jacobs reached into a bag and pulled out two shiny medals on blue ribbons. "Amelia and Sam, here's a medal for each of you for being such brilliant puppy trainers."

Everyone clapped as Mr Jacobs put the medals around their necks.

"Well done!" cheered Tiffany.

Then Mr Jacobs pulled out a dog treat. "And here's a reward for you, Coco. Congratulations."

Coco gobbled up her treat, her brown tail excitedly thumping the ground.

"Tiffany, this is for you," said Mr Jacobs,

putting a medal around her neck. "Well done for realising what it takes to be a good dog owner … and for not giving up."

"Yay, Tiffany!" cheered Sam.

Amelia clapped her hands. "Go Tiffany!"

Mr Jacobs gave Sparkle a treat too, and the little puppy scoffed it down.

Everyone laughed.

"What a great puppy party," said Sam, after Mr Jacobs had given out all of the medals.

And best of all, no fireworks, thought Amelia. *Or thunder!*

After the party, Amelia and Sam took Coco to Animal Ark for a check-up. In the examination room, Mrs Hope checked Coco's bite wound. Amelia could see that the scabs on Coco's leg had gone and the bite marks had faded.

"I'm pleased with her progress," said Mrs Hope. "The wound's nearly healed."

"Just in time!" said Sam. "Auntie Jen is coming to collect Coco later this afternoon."

"Does this mean Coco doesn't have to wear the cone any more?" asked Amelia.

Mrs Hope smiled. "That's right."

Amelia and Sam held the puppy, while Mrs Hope slipped the cone off her neck. Coco licked the vet, as if to say "thank you".

"She's one happy pup!" said Sam.

Amelia laughed. "Now let's get her back to her owner!"

When Auntie Jen arrived at the Old Mill that afternoon, Amelia and Sam proudly showed her what Coco had learned at puppy training classes.

"Call her, Auntie Jen," said Sam, as they watched Coco playing with Mac on the lawn. "She'll come right to you."

"Coco!" called Auntie Jen. "Here, Coco!"

Coco stopped when she heard her name and ran across the grass. Sam and Amelia showed Auntie Jen how Coco walked on the lead and played with her toys.

"Well done!" said Auntie Jen, tickling Coco under the chin. "You know exactly what to do now, don't you?"

"But that's not even the best bit," said Amelia.

Sam told Auntie Jen how Coco had helped to rescue Sparkle.

"Amazing!" Auntie Jen gave her

 puppy a cuddle. "That was really brave of you. But fast-flowing water can be very dangerous."

Amelia blushed. "We were really worried about Sparkle," she said.

"Of course," Auntie Jen said, smiling. "But you should never put your own lives at risk."

Amelia and Sam nodded solemnly.

All too soon, it was time for Auntie Jen and Coco to go home.

"I'm going to miss you, Coco," said

Amelia. She wrapped her arms around the puppy and gave her a cuddle. Coco licked her face.

Sam ruffled Coco's ears and tickled her under the chin. "See you soon, Coco. Be good."

"Thanks so much for training Coco," said Auntie Jen, as Coco and Mac chased each other around the lawn one last time. "I'll bring her back for another visit very soon."

Amelia stood outside the Old Mill with Sam, his parents and Mac. They all waved goodbye as Auntie Jen and Coco drove away.

"I'm kind of tired now," said Sam.

"Training Coco was fun – but hard work!"

"Should we ring the Hopes and say we can't come to Animal Ark tomorrow?" asked Amelia.

Sam's eyebrows shot up. "Are you serious?"

His expression was so funny that Amelia couldn't keep a straight face. "Only joking!"

"Phew!" said Sam, looking relieved.

Amelia burst out laughing and Sam joined in. *Nothing could keep us away from Animal Ark*, she thought. *We both love animals too much!*

The End

Read on for a sneak peek at Amelia and Sam's next adventure!

ANIMAL ARK

Lost Kitten

Lucy Daniels

"That must be it!" Amelia said. The grassy path that she and Sam were following disappeared into a tangle of bushes ahead, and she quickened her pace. "Gran said the wilderness is full of animals. I can't wait to see it!"

Suddenly, Sam's Westie puppy, Mac, let out an excited yip and strained at his leash. A fluffy white kitten sat washing its paws in the shadow of a bramble bush.

"Leave it!" Sam told Mac.

Amelia smiled as Mac planted his bottom and waited, looking up at Sam expectantly. *His training is really coming along!* she thought proudly.

The kitten didn't seem to notice Mac

at all. Amelia kneeled and held her hand towards it. "Hello, you," she said. The little cat looked up at her with wide blue eyes. "Awww! You are so cute!" Amelia said. The kitten stretched up on its back legs and butted its head into her fingers. Then it let out a loud *MIAOOOW!*

Mac whimpered.

"It's just a kitten, Mac," Sam said, grinning. "You can't be scared!" But Mac scrabbled behind Sam, eyeing the kitten warily.

Amelia scratched the kitten behind the ears and it started to purr, almost as loudly as Amelia's dad snored. She couldn't help giggling.

Sam led his puppy towards the thicket, giving the kitten a wide berth. "Let's explore!" he said.

Amelia felt a pang as she left the kitten behind. But when she glanced back she saw it happily batting at a fly, its blue saucer eyes darting in all directions. She followed Sam, pushing through twisted branches.

They soon broke out into an area of open, sunlit scrubland. A few tall, knobbly oaks grew from the undergrowth, but most of the trees were saplings. Wildflowers and long grass smothered the ground, and insects and feathery seeds filled the air, making everything look hazy and golden.

Sam unclipped the lead from Mac's collar. "Off you go!" The puppy tore away, hurtling through the long grass with his ears back and his tail stuck out behind him.

"This place is amazing!" Amelia said, taking it all in. Then she frowned. "Or it *would* be, if there wasn't so much rubbish." She could see at least half a dozen drinks cans on the ground, along with crisp packets, plastic bottles and even a dirty old sock.

A buzz from near Amelia's feet made her look down, just in time to see a bee zip out from a small hole in the sun-baked earth. "Look! A bumblebee's nest!" she said, pointing. But her excitement changed to dismay as the bee buzzed straight towards one of the empty drink cans. Amelia quickly turned it over, so the bee couldn't get stuck inside. "This place is such a mess!"

"You're right," Sam said, watching his puppy dive out of sight between two huge bushes. "I hope Mac doesn't eat something he shouldn't. We'd better keep an eye on him." Sam pushed his way through the branches after his little dog. Amelia followed close behind, stomping down on brambles that snagged at her trousers.

"Whoa!" Sam said. "Look at this!"

Mac was sniffing at the wall of a small rectangular building, half covered in ivy. The top part was decorated with wooden slats covered in peeling white paint and it had a peaked roof that made Amelia think of gingerbread houses. It *must* have been nice once, she thought. But now branches poked up through the roof-tiles and graffiti covered the brickwork.

Amelia peered in through the dark, gaping window hole. Part of the roof had fallen in, and weeds grew up through the rubble.

"What is this place?" Sam asked.

"I don't know," Amelia said. "But it's kind of spooky."

"Hello!" a deep male voice boomed from behind them. Amelia and Sam whirled around. Their classmate Tiffany and her father, Mr Banks, were walking down the wide grassy path that ran in front of the building. Trotting ahead of Tiffany on a short lead came Sparkle, her little curly-haired white dog. Tiffany munched on a chocolate bar, ignoring them.

"Hi there!" called Sam.

Amelia dropped to one knee to pet Sparkle, just as Mac bounded up to say hello. Tiffany rolled her eyes as the two dogs circled each other, sniffing.

"So, you've found the old signal box!" Mr Banks said. He pointed to a sign sticking up from a ledge of crumbling concrete. It was green with moss, but Amelia could just make out the words *Welford Station*.

"I didn't know there was a railway station in Welford!" said Amelia.

"Oh, it shut years before you were born," Mr Banks said, smiling.

Read **The Lost Kitten** to find out what happens next...

Animal Advice

Do you love animals as much as Amelia and Sam? Here are some tips on how to look after them from veterinary surgeon Sarah McGurk.

Caring for your pet

1. Animals need clean water at all times.
2. They need to be fed too – ask your vet what kind of food is best, and how much the animal needs.
3. Some animals, such as dogs, need exercise every da
4. Animals also need lots of love. You should always be very gentle with your pets and be careful not to c anything that might hurt them.

When to go to the vet

ometimes animals get ill. Like you, they will mostly get

etter on their own. But if your pet has hurt itself or

ems very unwell, then a trip to the vet might be needed.

me pets also need to be vaccinated, to prevent them

om getting dangerous diseases. Your vet can tell you

at your pet needs.

Helping wildlife

Always ask an adult before you go near any animals

you don't know.

If you find an animal or bird which is injured or can't

move, it is best not to touch it.

If you are worried, you can phone an animal charity

such as the RSPCA (SSPCA in Scotland) for help.

ANIMAL ARK

Where animals need you!

COLLECT ALL OF AMELIA AND SAM'S EXCITING ADVENTURES!